ETAN BORITZER is the bestselling children's book author of the *What is?* series, now published in 16 languages. Etan was first published when he was 13 years old and wrote an essay about his experience in his school classroom on the day that John F. Kennedy was assassinated. The essay was published in a New York City Public Schools anthology tribute to the slain president. Etan has also written screenplays for movies and TV shows, science fiction, art criticism, newspaper and magazine articles, plus numerous letters to the editor—some of which were actually published! When he is not writing by the beach near his home in Marina del Rey, California, Etan also helps other authors get published, and he travels to elementary schools around the country to do author visits, read from his books and teach his popular *Young Writers Workshop*. Etan is also a respected and longtime yoga teacher, and a philanthropist. He believes, as Audrey Hepburn said when she was UNESCO Goodwill Ambassador, "Children are the only hope."

SONAL GOYAL is based in Delhi, India and received her Masters in Fine Art from College of Art, Delhi. She has worked for major Indian publishing houses on various national and international illustration and art projects. Sonal now works independently from her own studio illustrating children's books and working on magazine projects with Indian and global clients. Sonal likes to work in different styles and media, including animation.

V **L** **B** **Veronica Lane Books**   www.veronicalanebooks.com
2554 Lincoln Blvd #142   •   Venice, CA 90291 USA   •   tel: (800) 651-1001
email: etan@veronicalanebooks.com

What is Respect?

By Etan Boritzer   Illustrated by Sonal Goyal

Veronica Lane Books

www.veronicalanebooks.com   email: etan@veronicalanebooks.com
2554 Lincoln Blvd. Ste 142, Los Angeles, CA 90291 USA
Tel: +1 (800) 651-1001

Library of Congress Cataloging-In-Publication Data
    Boritzer, Etan, 1950-
    What Is Respect / by Etan Boritzer
    Illustrated by Sonal Goyal -- 1st Edition
    p. cm.

SUMMARY: An exploration of various factors that make for self-respect and healthy social interactions.

Audience: Grades K - 6

Softbound ISBN 978-09910083-7-7
Hardbound ISBN 978-09910083-4-6

... to the children of the world ...

*W*hat is Respect?

Is respect an idea or a thing,
or is respect something that we do?

Where do we find respect?
Do we find respect at school,
at home, with our friends,
out in nature, or inside ourselves?

Why should we even ask *What is Respect?*
Because our parents or our teachers tell us
that we need to know what respect is?

Who should we respect?
And is there anybody or anything
that we should not respect?

You see, there are lots of questions
that are part of this big question,
What is Respect?
so let's find out what it really means.

*W*e know that our parents and teachers
use the word *respect* a lot,
and that it is really important to them.

Why do you think that is?
Maybe parents and teachers want us
to learn what respect means
so that we become more caring and kind
to our friends and families,
to other people that we just meet,
and even to plants and animals.

Maybe if we learn what respect is,
then we can also start to *practice* respect.

And if we practice respect,
we may get really good at it,
and people will feel our respect,
and that will make them feel good,
and then they'll respect us,
and soon there will be more caring,
and more kindness,
and more respect everywhere!

*W*hat is Respect?

The dictionary says that respect is a feeling,
a feeling of high value or worth
that you have for somebody or something
because you care about them.

What does *that* mean?
It means you feel that somebody or something
is special or precious,
meaning hard to find or replace.

Respect means you feel that
somebody or something is important,
that you really appreciate them,
and that you are careful not to hurt them,
or treat them badly.

Respect means we have to be careful
of what we say to people,
what we do to people
and even what we think about people.

Respect means you have to be sensitive
to what others are feeling,
so that everybody is happy
and nobody feels hurt.

Respect means to care!

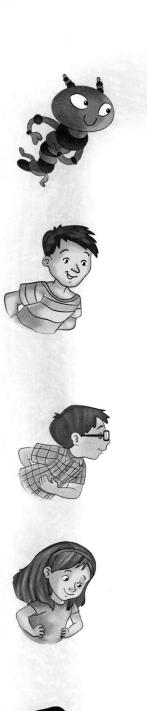

Who should we respect?

We know that we should respect
our family and friends,
and that we should treat them very special.
But do we always do that?

Should we respect people from other places
who don't speak our language?
Should we respect people
who have a different skin color than we do,
or are of a different religion than we are?
Or, who dress differently than we do,
or who eat different food than we do?

Should we respect people who work for us?
Like your school bus driver,
or the lady who serves you lunch,
or the people who work for your parents?

Should we respect somebody
that we just meet for the first time?
Should we respect homeless people,
or homeless kids, or homeless families?

Should we respect differently-abled kids?
Should we respect kids who are really sick,
or kids who learn differently,
or kids with attention or behavior problems?

Should we respect dead people?

*S*hould you respect somebody
when they don't respect you, like if
somebody says something hurtful to you,
or something about you that is not true?

Should you respect somebody
when they don't share a treat,
or invite you to their party,
or they put their hands on you?

Should you respect somebody
when you let them use your things,
like your clothes or games
and they don't respect your things?

Should you respect somebody
when they don't respect your time,
or don't respect something you did for them?

Should you respect somebody
when they make fun of your weight,
or the way you walk, or make fun of your name,
or tease you about other stuff that
they think is funny, but you don't?

When somebody does not respect you,
what should you do?

*S*hould you respect somebody
who disturbs others in class?

Should you respect somebody
who doesn't get good grades?
Should you respect somebody
who is not good at sports?

Should you respect somebody
who smells bad,
or who does not wear new clothes?
Should you respect a bully?

Should you respect somebody
who is your friend one day,
and then the next day they tell you,
You're not my friend anymore!

When you don't respect somebody,
what happens to that person?
When you don't respect somebody,
what happens to *you*?

Maybe a person says or does something
that is hurtful and not respectful
to your feelings, to your body or to your things.

Maybe that person says or does it by mistake,
or maybe on purpose.

Is that person really a bad person?

A person who hurts others or is not respectful,
has been hurt by others.
Can you try to understand or forgive that person?

If a person hurts you or is not respectful to you,
maybe you can express your feelings to that person.

How do you do that?
First, take a couple of breaths.

Then, look the person in the eye and say,
"*That hurt me. Don't ever say or do that again.*"

Then you can say, "*I forgive you.*"

*I*f that doesn't work,
and the person does not stop hurting you,
you can yell real loud, *NO!!!*
Let's practice that together right now.
Let's all say *NO!!!* together, at the count of three.
Ready? One, two, three – *NO!!!*

You might even have to yell *NO!!!*
more than once, maybe two or three times
until that person really stops saying or doing
that thing that is hurting you
and not respecting you.

If that doesn't work,
walk away from that person and tell an adult
like your Mom or Dad, or a teacher, or a counselor,
or another family member, or a neighbor,
or a friend, or a friend's Mom or Dad,
or even a policewoman, or policeman.

And maybe because you answered
that person with respect, even strong respect,
maybe now they will learn to respect other people,
and maybe they'll also learn to respect themselves.

How do we respect people?

We respect people
when we don't hurt their bodies or their feelings,
or their things.

We respect people by speaking to them
in a polite, kind and caring way.

We respect people by thinking about them
in a kind and caring way.

We respect people
when we put a high value on everybody we meet,
every day and every moment and everywhere.
And when we respect people,
most of the time they will respect us.

We respect people
when we understand that most people
have the same feelings that we do,
happy feelings and sad feelings,
love feelings and hurt feelings.

We respect people
when we understand that we all have to live together
in our neighborhood and on our planet
in a happy and peaceful way.

*C*an we respect *things*?
Like our personal things, our clothes and books,
and our computers by taking care of them
so they don't get damaged?

Can we respect things
like the places we live in,
like our home, our street and our neighborhood,
by keeping things there clean and orderly?

Can we respect other people's things
just like they are our things
by taking care of them and returning them on time?

Can we respect living things
like pets and animals on farms,
or animals out in nature,
even bugs like spiders,
by not killing them or disturbing them?

Can we respect living things
like the flowers and the plants and trees,
and all of the other beautiful things on planet earth,
like the oceans and rivers, and forests and deserts
and the mountains –
by keeping the earth clean and not polluted?

Can you respect dead things,
like a dead seagull on the beach?

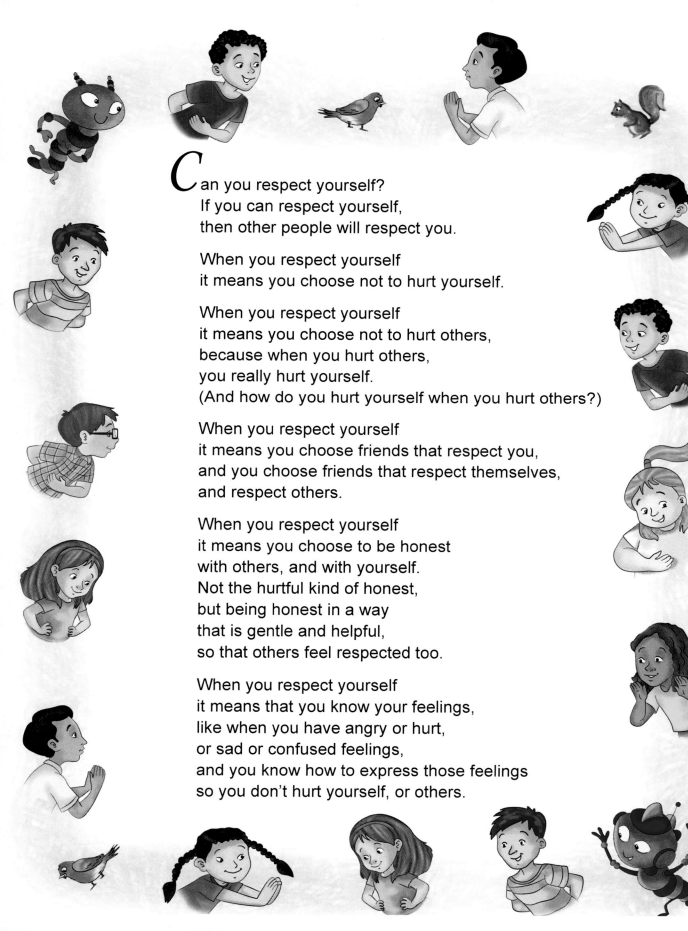

*C*an you respect yourself?
If you can respect yourself,
then other people will respect you.

When you respect yourself
it means you choose not to hurt yourself.

When you respect yourself
it means you choose not to hurt others,
because when you hurt others,
you really hurt yourself.
(And how do you hurt yourself when you hurt others?)

When you respect yourself
it means you choose friends that respect you,
and you choose friends that respect themselves,
and respect others.

When you respect yourself
it means you choose to be honest
with others, and with yourself.
Not the hurtful kind of honest,
but being honest in a way
that is gentle and helpful,
so that others feel respected too.

When you respect yourself
it means that you know your feelings,
like when you have angry or hurt,
or sad or confused feelings,
and you know how to express those feelings
so you don't hurt yourself, or others.

$\mathcal{H}$ow else can you respect yourself?
You can respect your body.

You can respect your body
by keeping it clean, and smelling nice.

You can respect your body
by eating healthy food,
not junk food that's fried, salty or sugary.
You can drink good water,
and *not* drink sodas or sugary stuff.

You can respect your body
by exercising regularly, doing sports,
or going out to the park or beach, or hiking
with your parents and friends,
and getting lots of fresh air.

You can respect your body
by not sitting around for hours
and playing violent video games.

You can respect your body
by not letting anyone touch it
who you don't want to touch it.

What other ways can you respect your body?

You can also respect yourself
by respecting your mind.
But how do you do that?

You can respect your mind
by feeding it good things.
But how do you do that?

You can respect your mind
by feeding it good books
that teach you good things
like being kind to others and being helpful.

You can respect your mind
by feeding it good TV shows,
good movies and good video games
that don't show hateful or ugly things,
but teach you how to be peaceful
and kind, and respectful to others.

You can respect your mind
by feeding it happy thoughts
about your family and friends,
not hurtful or angry thoughts.

But what can you do
if you are feeding your mind
hurtful or angry thoughts about yourself,
or about somebody else?

*I*f you are feeding your mind
hurtful or angry thoughts,
you can learn to meditate.

When you meditate
it means that you sit down in a place,
you start to breathe slowly
and slow down your mind
so you can start to calm down
any hurtful or angry thoughts
or feelings in the mind.

Maybe somebody hurt your feelings
by saying something about you
that is not true, or made fun of you
in front of the other kids.
Maybe somebody didn't do want you wanted.
Maybe you think somebody doesn't like you.

When you meditate you start to feed your mind
all the good things you know about yourself
and all the good things
that others know about you.

Soon those hurtful or angry thoughts and feelings
will start to fade away from your mind,
and you will feel peaceful and happy,
and you will feel your own self-respect again,
no matter what anybody else says or does.

*C*an you respect people of respect?

Besides ourselves, and family and friends,
and strangers, and animals and planet earth,
can you respect people of respect?

Sometimes people of respect wear uniforms
or other clothes than we do
because they belong to groups
that think and act with respect.

We see these people all around us,
and we believe that we can respect them.
But even if a person wears a uniform
or some other clothes of respect,
how do we know that we can really respect them?

Maybe if we watch those people real close,
and if we listen to them real close,
we can see and know
from their words and actions
if they really deserve our respect.

And if those people with uniforms
don't act with respect toward us or other people,
what can we do?

What is Respect?

Respect is caring for yourself,
and for others, and for things,
both living things and just stuff.

Respect is caring for our bodies and minds.
Respect is caring about other people's
bodies and minds and feelings,
through our kind actions, words and thoughts.

Respect is caring about people,
even if they sometimes don't respect us,
because we know that sometimes people are afraid,
or have been hurt,
and they want to hurt somebody else to get even.
But we still have to try to help those people
to understand respect.

Respect is living together,
caring for this beautiful earth
with all its plants, animals, fish, birds, bugs,
(and yes, even with spiders),
with all kinds of boys and girls, and people,
and yes, maybe even with aliens!

And now we understand that everybody
and everything likes and needs respect,
and that respect is caring.